TO MY FAMILY FOR TEACHING ME THE IMPORTANCE OF LAUGHTER,
AND TO MY PUG DOG, WHO MADE ME LAUGH EVERY SINGLE DAY.
—P.C.

FOR CHARLIE AND LOGAN WHO, LIKE ME,
STILL THINK POTTY HUMOR IS THE BEST.
—M.H.

TEXT COPYRIGHT © 2019 POPPY CHAMPIGNON
ILLUSTRATIONS COPYRIGHT © 2019 MARK HOFFMANN
BOOK DESIGN BY MELISSA NELSON GREENBERG

LIBRARY OF CONGRESS CATALOGING-IN-PUBLICATION DATA AVAILABLE.

ISBN: 978-1-944903-74-9

PRINTED IN CHINA   10 9 8 7 6 5 4 3 2 1

CAMERON KIDS IS AN IMPRINT OF CAMERON + COMPANY

CAMERON + COMPANY
PETALUMA, CA 94952
WWW.CAMERONBOOKS.COM

POOP

POPPY CHAMPIGNON & MARK HOFFMANN

cameron kids

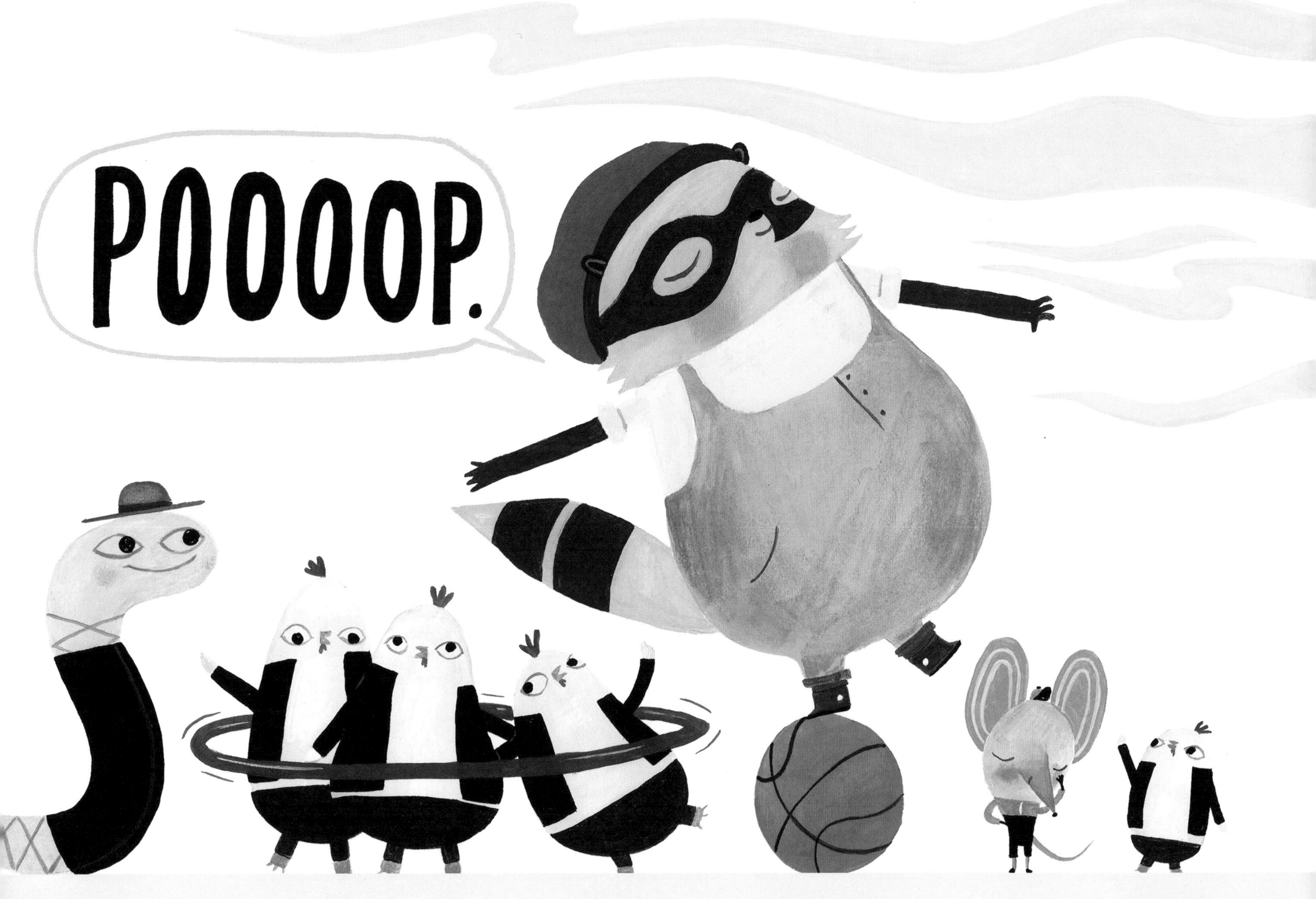
POOOOP.

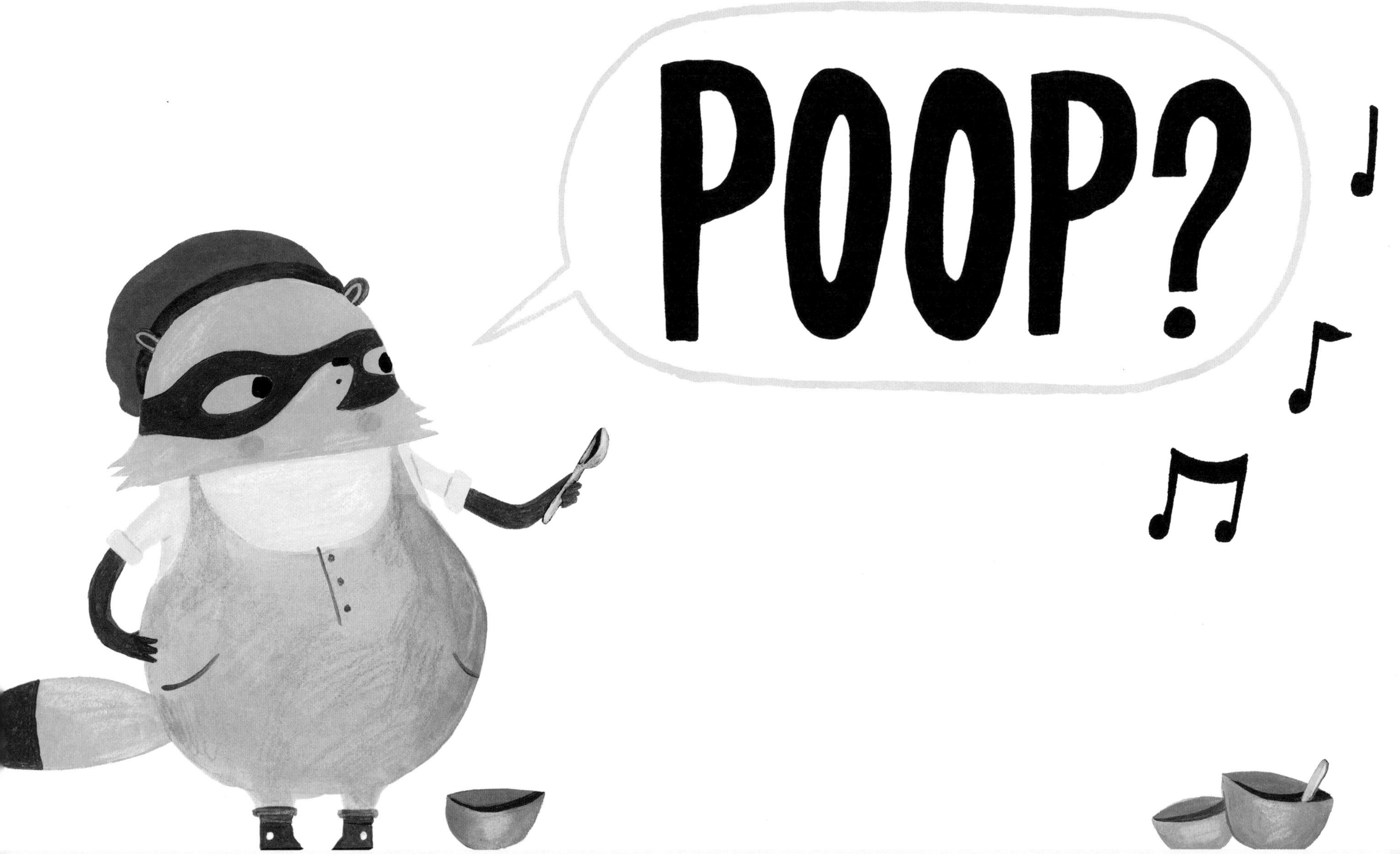
POOP?